CW00859876

Written by Patricia Attoe
Illustrated by Julia Ennis

Published in New York, New York

ISBN:
978-4-239-41225-4

This book
belongs to:

Name: _____

Date: _____

One chilly evening, Benjamin hears loud noises in his bedroom.

It is dark, Benjamin doesn't know where the noises are coming from, but they seem to be getting louder and louder. He imagines monsters in the wall, in his closet, under his bed!

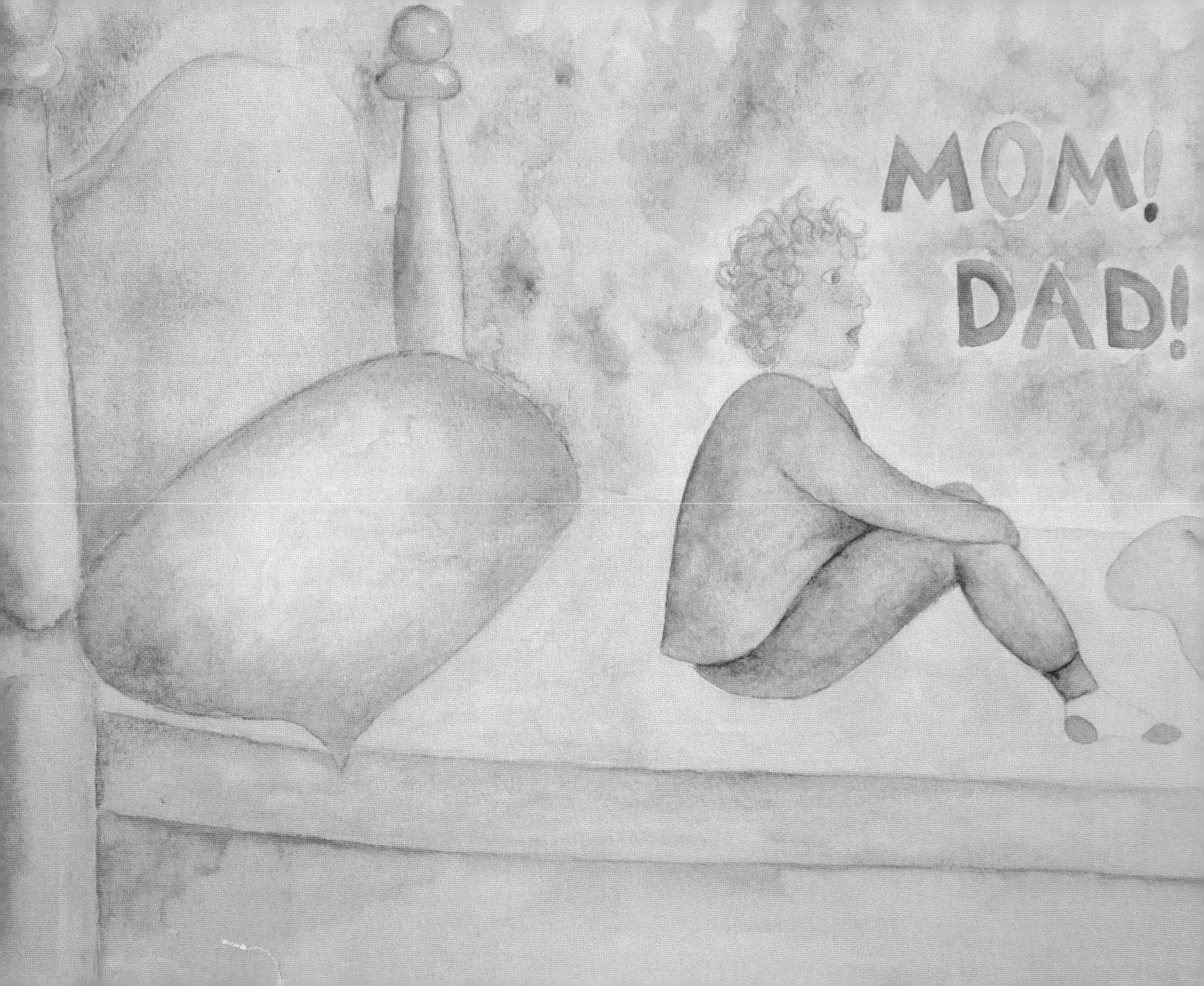
MOM!
DAD!

Benjamin's parents rush into his room. His father brings him a glass of water and his mother rocks him on her lap and wipes his tears.

"What's frightening you?" she asks.

BANG BANG
BANG!
CLANKITY
CLANG
CLANG
CLANG
HISsssssss

Benjamin yanks the covers over his head, "That noise!"

"There's nothing to be afraid of, Benjamin. That's just the radiator working to keep us warm," his father explains.

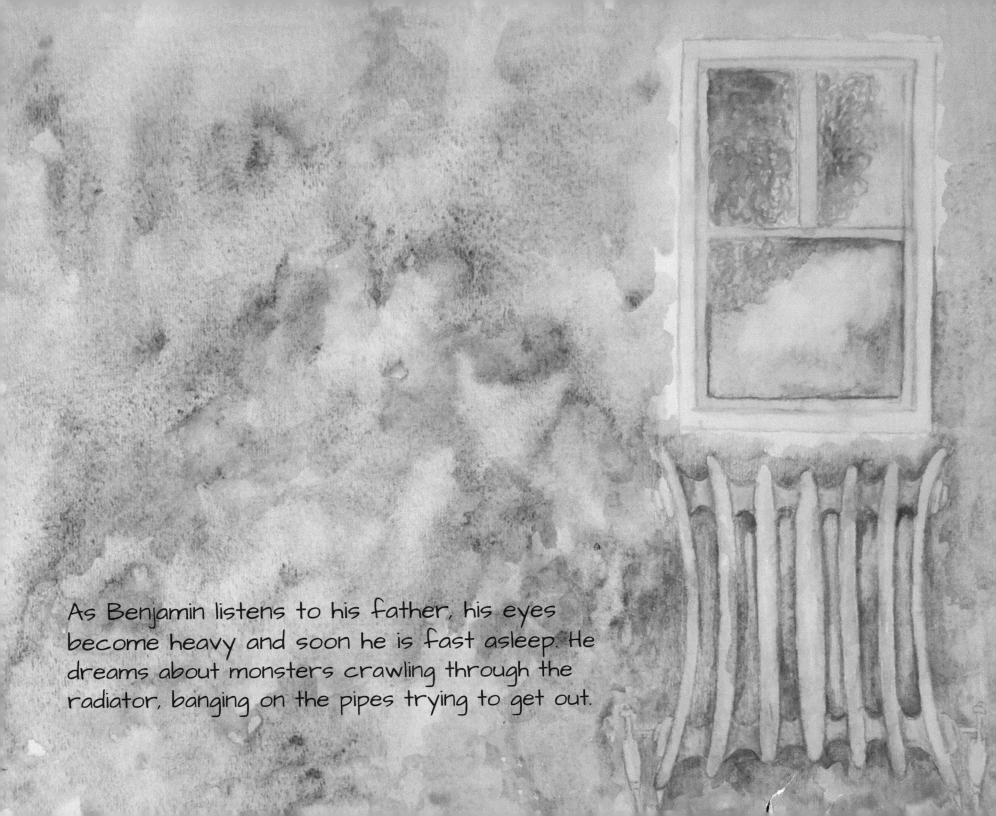

As Benjamin listens to his father, his eyes become heavy and soon he is fast asleep. He dreams about monsters crawling through the radiator, banging on the pipes trying to get out.

CLANKITY-
CLANKITY-
CLANG-CLANG
HISSSSSSSSS

Benjamin wakes up, startled. When he opens his eyes he is surprised to find a tiny boy with webbed feet standing on his nose.

"Who are you?" Benjamin asks.

"My name is Rusty."

"Where did you come from?"

"I live in the radiator."

"What are you doing here?"

Rusty yawns, "I was asleep, but I woke up when I heard you crying. What's wrong?"

"I was sleeping too, then I heard scary noises..."

BANG BANG BANG BANG

CLANKITY-CLANG-CLANG

HISSSSSSSSSSSSS

Benjamin dives under the covers. Rusty laughs. He laughs so hard that he loses his balance and tumbles down Benjamin's nose and lands on the bedsheets.

"What's so funny?" Benjamin wants to know as he peeks out from under his blanket.

Rusty covers his mouth to keep from laughing.
"That's just my dad."

"Your dad?"

"Come on, I'll show you."

Benjamin follows Rusty across the room to the radiator. He jumps when a burst of steam is released (HISS!), but relaxes when he sees that his new friend is not afraid.

Rusty climbs up the radiator and knocks three times on the metal pipes.

BANG! BANG! BANG!

Like an echo, the three knocks are returned from inside.

BANG! BANG! BANG!

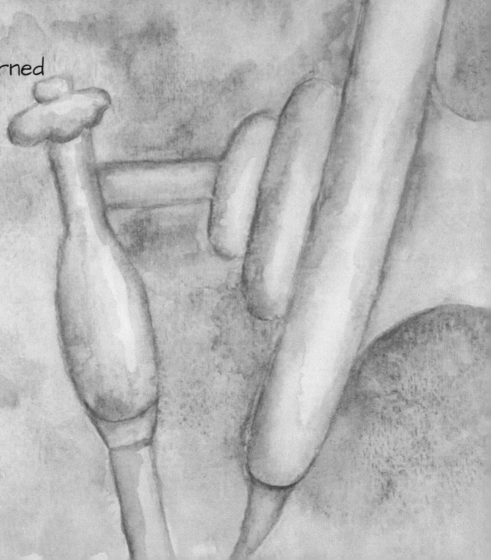

"Hi Dad!"

"Hello, son! Isn't it past your bedtime?"

Rusty quickly slides down the radiator, "Time for me to go."

"Wait!" Benjamin yells. "What's it like inside there?"

"It's very hot, dark and wet."

"How can you live in there with all that boiling water and steam? Isn't it dangerous?"

"No, not for radiator people. We love the heat and we're expert swimmers."

This time Benjamin is not afraid. "But what's all the noise?"

Rusty rubs his belly. "That's just mom and dad scraping rust off the pipes for breakfast tomorrow!"

"You eat rust?"

"Yup, I eat more rust than anyone in my family. That's why they call me Rusty."

BANG! BANG! BANG!

"Dad's calling again. I better be getting home."

"Will you visit again?" Benjamin asks hopefully.

"Sure. I'll tell mom and dad to keep it down so you can sleep. But don't be afraid, everyone has to blow off a little steam once in a while." Rusty waves before disappearing behind the radiator.

"Good night, Rusty!" Benjamin calls as he drifts off to sleep.

The next morning, Benjamin can't help
but tell his parents all about Rusty and the radiator people.
"They eat rust for breakfast!" he reports while nibbling his toast.

"What an imagination you have!" Benjamin's mother smiles. "You must have been dreaming. Now hurry up, the school bus will be here any minute."

Benjamin gathers his books, but before he leaves he yells, "Bye, Rusty!" He waits for a response.

Beep- Beep!

"The bus is here. Hurry!" His mother rushes him out the door.

Alone in the kitchen, Bejamin's parents suddenly hear a loud noise coming from inside the radiator.

BANG! BANG! BANG! CLANKITY- CLANG- CLANG! HISS!

Benjamin's parents' eyes widen,
"Radiator people?"

To Stephen, with love.

CPSIA information can be obtained
at www.ICGtesting.com
Printed in the USA
LVRC101611250821
696093LV00008B/105